For Mum and Dad, who made sure that Father Christmas always found me—J. R.

For the amazing Barney, Joshua, John, and Lydia, with love and thanks for being you—T. B.

Fletcher and the Snowflake Christmas. Text copyright © 2010 by Julia Rawlinson. Illustrations copyright © 2010 by Tiphanie Beeke. First published in 2010 in Great Britain by Gullane Children's Books as *Ferdie's Christmas*. First published in 2010 in the United States by Greenwillow Books. The right of Julia Rawlinson to be identified as the author and Tiphanie Beeke as the illustrator of this work has been asserted by them. All rights reserved. Manufactured in China. For information address HarperCollins Children's Books, 10 East 53rd Street, New York, NY 10022. www.harpercollinschildrens.com. Pastels were used to prepare the full-color art. The text type is Gloucester Old Style.

Library of Congress Cataloging-in-Publication Data:
Rawlinson, Julia. Fletcher and the snowflake Christmas / by Julia Rawlinson ; illustrated by Tiphanie Beeke. p. cm. "Greenwillow Books." Summary: At Christmastime, Fletcher the and the other forest animals lay a trail of sticks to help Santa find the rabbits' new burrow. ISBN 978-0-06-199033-5 (trade bdg.) [1. Foxes—Fiction. 2. Forest animals—Fiction. 3. Santa Claus—Fiction. 4. Christmas—Fiction. 5. Friendship—Fiction.] I. Beeke, Tiphanie, ill. II. Title. PZ7.R1974Flg 2010 [E]—dc22 2009042526

10 11 12 13 14 GBUK 10 9 8 7 6 5 4 3 2 1 First Edition  Greenwillow Books

# Fletcher
## and the
# Snowflake
# Christmas

BY JULIA RAWLINSON

PICTURES BY TIPHANIE BEEKE

GREENWILLOW BOOKS, AN IMPRINT OF HarperCollinsPublishers

It was an ice-bright Christmas Eve, and the sky was a dazzling blue. Every tree in the forest was frost-sprinkled and sparkling, and frozen puddles creaked and crackled under Fletcher's paws. He padded down the burrow bank to where the rabbits used to live, and bounced over the fallen tree that blocked their old front door.

And he stopped.

And he looked.

And he had a terrible thought . . .

How was Santa Claus going to find the rabbits' new home?

Fletcher shivered as a chill wind sliced through the forest,
rattling the bare branches. He thought about how sad he would
feel if he had to move from his cozy den. He thought about how
the rabbits would feel if Santa Claus did not come.
And then he thought about . . .

*arrows!*

Fletcher began to search around,
collecting sticks from the frosty
ground and arranging them to
make a trail of arrows leading
to the new burrow.

"What are you doing?" asked Squirrel,
looking down from the branches.
"Making a trail to show Santa Claus the way
to the rabbits' new burrow," said Fletcher.
"Otherwise they might not get their presents,"
gasped Squirrel, and he scampered down
to help Fletcher collect more sticks.

Soon a flock of birds gathered in the treetops, their feathers fluffed against the cold, to see what was going on.

"We're making a trail to the rabbits' new burrow," said Fletcher.

"For Santa Claus," added Squirrel.

"We'll help you!" chirped the birds.

The trail passed between bare trees and crossed the tinkling, ice-edged stream. The sun began to set, turning the sky a dazzling gold. Fletcher and Squirrel shivered and hurried up the little hill to where the mice were draping their nest with leaves of holly and ivy.

"What are you doing?" asked the mice.

"We're making a trail,"
said Fletcher.

"To the rabbits'
new burrow,"
said Squirrel.

"For Santa Claus,"
added the birds.

"You'd better hurry,"
said the mice. "It's
getting late. We'll help
you!"

So Fletcher, Squirrel, the birds, and the mice finished the trail to the rabbits' new home, which was cozy and warm and sweet with the smell of blackberry pie. They gathered around the crackling fire, thawing out their icy noses, nibbling pieces of pie, and singing Christmas songs. And while Squirrel put on a juggling show with holly berries and mistletoe, outside in the shivery darkness . . .

it began to snow.
Fat white flakes tumbled softly from a heavy sky.

They landed light and whisper quiet on the frozen ground.

When Fletcher went to the burrow door to go home for the night, the snow was soft and deep and white, and all the arrows were gone.

"Oh, no!" cried Fletcher, blinking back tears.

"What will happen to your presents now? Santa Claus will never be able to find your home."

Fletcher stared out into the darkness,
imagining Santa Claus lost in the snow.

"I have an idea," Fletcher said, gathering his friends. "If we stay awake tonight, when Santa Claus visits *our* homes, we can tell him how to find the rabbits' new home."

The animals said good night to one another and hurried off through the snow-muffled forest.

Fletcher snuggled down in his warm,
soft bed to keep watch for Santa Claus.

But . . .
curled in the cozy hollow
of an oak tree, Squirrel
began to snore.

High in the snowy
branches of a fir tree,
the birds began to doze.

In their toasty warm
nest, the mice dreamed
of berries wrapped
with ribbons.

And in his snug little bed,
Fletcher's eyes closed.
So when Santa Claus
came to call, everyone was
fast asleep.
But the next morning,
when Fletcher rushed to
the rabbits' burrow . . .

Santa Claus had found it after all!
"I'm sorry I went to sleep," puffed Fletcher,
"but I've brought you a Christmas rose."
"And we've brought nuts," panted Squirrel,
carrying the mice through the snow.
"And we've brought berries," sang the birds.

"And best of all, you've brought yourselves,
and there's room in the burrow for everyone,"
said the rabbits.

"Merry Christmas!" cried the rabbits,
and they welcomed their friends into
the berry-bright warmth of their home.